SHOCK FOREST

AND OTHER STORIES

Margaret Mahy

illustrated by Wendy Smith

A & C Black • London

White Wolves Series Consultant: Sue Ellis, Centre for Literacy in Primary Education

This book can be used in the White Wolves Guided Reading
programme with Year 6 pupils who are achieving reading independence.

First published 2004 by
A & C Black Publishers Ltd
37 Soho Square, London, W1D 3QZ

www.acblack.com

"Shock Forest" first appeared in *Beyond the Rainbow Warrior,* edited by Michael
Morpurgo, © Margaret Mahy 1996. Published by Chrysalis Children's Books.
"Rooms to Let" first appeared in *Leaf Magic and Five Other Favourites*,
© Margaret Mahy 1976, 1984. First published by J.M. Dent and Sons.
"The House of Coloured Windows" and "The Bridge Builder" first appeared in
The Door in the Air and Other Stories, © Margaret Mahy 1988. First published by
J.M. Dent and Sons. "The Travelling Boy and the Stay At Home Bird" first appeared
in *The Chewing-Gum Rescue,* © 1982. First published by J.M. Dent and Sons.

The rights of Margaret Mahy and Wendy Smith to be identified as author and
illustrator of this work respectively have been asserted by them in accordance
with the Copyrights, Designs and Patents Act 1988.

ISBN 0-7136-7027-4

A CIP catalogue for this book is available from the British Library.

A&C Black uses paper produced with elemental chlorine-free
pulp, harvested from managed sustained forests.

Printed and bound in Spain by G. Z. Printek, Bilbao.

To Alice and Poppy –
once again

CONTENTS

THE HOUSE OF COLOURED WINDOWS

Our street had a lot of little houses on either side of it where we children lived happily with our families. There were rows of lawns, like green napkins tucked under the houses' chins, and letterboxes, apple trees and marigolds. Children played up and down the street, laughing and shouting and sometimes crying, for it's the way of the world that things should be mixed. In the soft autumn evenings, before the winter winds began, the smoke from chimneys rose up in threads of grey and blue, stitching our houses into the autumn air.

But there was one house in our street that was different from all the rest, and that was the wizard's house. For one thing there was a door knocker of iron in the shape of a dog's head that barked at us as we ran by. Of course, the wizard's house had its lawn too, but no apple trees or marigolds, only a silver tree with a golden parrot in it. But that was not the most wonderful thing about the wizard's house.

The real wonders of the wizard's house were its windows. They were all the colours of the world – red, blue, green, gold, purple and pink, violet and yellow, as well as the reddish-brown of autumn leaves. His house was patched all over with coloured windows. And there was not just one pink window or one green one, either, but several of each colour, each one different. No one had told us but we all knew that if you looked through the red window you saw a red world. If you looked through the blue window a blue one. The wizard could go into any of these worlds whenever he wished. He was not only the owner of many windows, but the master of many worlds.

My friend, Anthea, longed to go into the wizard's house and spy out through his windows. Other people dreamed of racing-bikes and cameras and guitars, but Anthea dreamed of the wizard's windows. She wanted to get into the wizard's house and look through first one window and then another because she was sure that through one of them she must see the world she really wanted to live in. The candyfloss window would show her a world

10

striped like circus time, the golden window would show her a city of towers and domes, dazzling in the sunlight, and every girl who lived there would be a princess with long golden hair. The windows haunted Anthea so much that her eyes ached for magic peep-holes into strange and beautiful countries.

One day, as Anthea came home from school she saw on the footpath outside the wizard's house, sitting by his letterbox, a white cat with one blue eye and one green eye, golden whiskers and a collar of gold. It winked at her with its blue eye and scrambled through a gap in the hedge, seeming to beckon with its tail. Anthea scrambled after it with a twist and a wriggle and, when she stood up, she was on the other side of the hedge inside the wizard's garden. Her school uniform had been changed into a long, silver dress with little glass bells all over its sleeves, and her school shoes and socks had changed into slippers of scarlet and stockings of green. In front of her stood the wizard, dressed in a white robe with a tiny green dragon crawling around his shoulders. His cat rubbed against his ankles and purred.

"So, you are the girl who dreams of looking through my windows," said the wizard. "Your wishes are like storms, my dear – too strong, too strong. At night I am beginning to dream your dreams instead of my own and that won't do, for wizards need their own dreams to prevent them becoming lost in their magic. Dreams are to wizards what harbour lights are to a sailor. I'll let you look through my windows, and choose the world you like best of all, so long as you remember that when you walk out of my door you'll walk out into the world you have chosen, and there'll be no coming back a second time. Be sure you choose well."

Anthea followed the wizard up the path between borders of prize-winning geraniums and in at his door.

"This is a lovely dress," she said to the wizard. "I feel halfway to being a princess already. It's much, much nicer than my school uniform."

"But it *is* a school uniform – the uniform of

my school," the wizard replied in surprise. "I'm glad you like it. Now, here is the red window. Look well, my dear."

Anthea looked through the red window. She was looking deep into a forest on the sun. Trees blazed up from a wide plain and over a seething hillside. Their leaves were flames, and scarlet smoke rose up from the forest, filling the sky. Out from under the trees galloped a herd of fiery horses, tossing burning manes and tails and striking sparks from the ground with their smouldering hooves.

"Well?" asked the wizard.

"It's beautiful," breathed Anthea, "but it's much too hot."

The next window was a silver one. A princess, with a young face and long white hair, rode through a valley of snow in a silver sleigh drawn by six great white bears wearing collars of frost and diamonds. All around her, mountains rose like needles of silver ice into a blue, clear sky.

"Your silver window is beautiful," Anthea sighed, "but, oh – how cold, how cold! I couldn't live there."

Through a candyfloss-pink window, sure enough, she looked into a world of circuses. A pink circus tent opened like a spring tree in blossom. Clowns turned cartwheels around it, and a girl in a pink dress and pink slippers rode on a dappled horse, jumping through a hoop hung with pink ribbons.

"That's funny!" Anthea said in a puzzled voice. "It's happy and funny and very, very pretty, but I wouldn't want to live with a circus every day. I don't know why not but I just wouldn't."

That's how it was with all the windows. The blue one looked under the sea, and the green one into a world of treetops. There was a world of deserts and a world of diamonds, a world of caves and glow-worms, and a world of sky with floating cloud-castles, but Anthea did not want to live in any of them. She began to run from one window to another, the glass bells on her sleeves jingling and tinkling, her feet in the scarlet slippers sliding under her.

"Where is a window for me?" cried Anthea.

She peered through windows into lavender worlds full of mist, worlds where grass grew up to the sky and spiders spun bridges with rainbow-coloured silk, into worlds where nothing grew and where great stones lay like a city of abandoned castles reaching from one horizon to another.

At last there were no windows left. The wizard's house had many, many windows, but Anthea had looked through them all and there was no world in which she wanted to live. She didn't want a hot one or a cold one, a wet one or a dry one. She didn't want a world of trees or a world of stones. The wizard shrugged his shoulders.

"You're hard to please," he said.

"But I wanted the very best one. I know I'd know the best one if only you'd let me see it. Isn't there one window left? One little window?"

"Funnily enough there is one window, but I didn't think you'd be interested," the wizard said. "You see ..."

"Please show it to me," begged Anthea.

"I ought to explain ..." began the wizard.

"Please!" cried Anthea.

15

The wizard pointed at a little blue-and-white checked curtain. "Behind there," he said.

Anthea ran to pull it aside and found herself looking through a window as clear as a drop of rain water. She saw a little street with little houses on either side of it. Smoke went up, up, up, stitching the street into the autumn sky, and up and down the footpath children ran, shouting and laughing, though some were also crying. There was a woman very like Anthea's own mother, looking for someone very like Anthea, because dinner was ready and there were sausages and mashed potatoes waiting to be eaten.

"That's the one!" cried Anthea, delighted. "Why did you keep it until last? I've wasted a lot of time on other windows when this one was the best all the time."

Without waiting another moment, she ran out of the wizard's door, squeezed through the hedge and found herself in the street wearing her own school uniform again.

"Well, that's funny!" said the wizard to his

cat. "Did you see that? She went back to the world she came out of in the first place. That's her mother taking her home for dinner. I must say they do look very happy."

Ten minutes later the white cat with the gold collar brought him a tray with his dinner on it. The wizard looked pleased.

"Oh boy!" he said, because he was having sausages and mashed potatoes, too.

And that night the wizard dreamed his own dreams once more, while Anthea dreamed of a racing-bike. And in the darkness, the wizard's house of many windows twinkled like a good spell amid the street lights that marched like bright soldiers down our street.

ROOMS TO LET

Mr Murgatroyd hung a sign on the front door of his house: ROOMS TO LET.

He was small and shrivelled and as bitter as medicine because of the mean, hard life he had led, and he talked to himself because of his loneliness.

"How much shall I charge for my rooms?" he asked himself. He chuckled. "*Too* much!" he declared so sharply that the key rattled in the lock, probably from fear.

One day Mr Murgatroyd heard an unusual-sounding knock on the door. It was a light, soft knock, as if a bird was tapping with its claw. Mr Murgatroyd listened, turning down the corners of his mouth. Finally he went to the door and opened it.

There stood a little, wispy woman, vague as thistledown, her nose pink at the tip and her hair a bit stringy around her ears. "I would like to live in one of your rooms," she said shyly.

"Come this way," said Mr Murgatroyd.

Shuffle-tap, shuffle-tap, went the old

21

woman's footsteps. (She had a wooden leg.)

"I should warn you that I'm going to charge too much," Mr Murgatroyd said crossly.

The woman sighed a rustly sigh. "That is what I always have to pay," she said.

Mr Murgatroyd showed her to her room and left her there. As he was going back down the stairs, he heard another knock at the door (just an ordinary knock, this time). He grinned and slid like a wicked shadow to open it. There stood a man with a mermaid in a wheelbarrow.

"Have you rooms?" the man asked.

"I have," said Mr Murgatroyd.

The mermaid smiled at him through her net of yellow hair, and Mr Murgatroyd blushed.

"We will take one," the man said. "We will have a room with a bathroom. My wife likes a bathroom."

"You have to share the bathroom," said Mr Murgatroyd quickly. "There's only one."

"Then we'll have a room right next to it," declared the man triumphantly.

Mr Murgatroyd shuffled his feet uneasily.

"I ought to mention that the rent is too much," he said nervously.

"My dear fellow, it's always too much, isn't it?" the man replied.

Mr Murgatroyd went back to his room. He did not look so sure of himself any more. A crack in the ceiling grinned down at him. The wind outside laughed and rattled his windows. "Things aren't going to be as easy as I thought," Mr Murgatroyd said to himself.

"Knock, knock," went his front door again. Mr Murgatroyd got wearily to his feet and went back to open it. Outside stood Mrs Piper looking like a rainbow, all patched and stitched, while behind her, hanging on to her left hand and her right hand and stretching far down the street, were twenty children, all stitched and patched too.

"Ah, Mr Murgatroyd, dear," said Mrs Piper, "I see you've rooms to let."

"No children allowed!" cried Mr Murgatroyd, seizing the door handle anxiously. "Anyhow, I charge too much!" he warned her.

Mrs Piper blinked.

"Not even if I pay much too much?" she asked. Mr Murgatroyd could not resist the thought of much too much.

"All right," he said. "All right! But you see that you keep those brats of yours in order, Mrs Piper, or the house won't be worth living in."

"Oh, a few children make a house homey," said Mrs Piper, and she shooed her scrambling, rambling family, with Mr Murgatroyd leading, to the big rooms at the back of the house.

Finally there was only one room left. Who would come for that? Mr Murgatroyd scrunched his head down between his shoulders.

Now he had: a wispy little woman with a wooden leg; a man who pushed his mermaid wife in a wheelbarrow; Mrs Piper and her twenty children.

There's nobody much left who could surprise me, thought Mr Murgatroyd.

"Knock, knock," went the door.

Mr Murgatroyd opened it only a crack.

There stood a large, black bear.

"Good evening," said the bear.

Mr Murgatroyd wanted to shut the door but he was afraid the bear might beat it in with his huge paws.

"What do you want?" he whispered.

"A room," said the bear. "I'm learning to play the flute. I need a small, quiet, plain room suitable for fluting in."

"I charge too much," Mr Murgatroyd said, still in a whisper.

"Curious!" the bear remarked. "I always pay too much."

He marched inside and peered with small bear-eyes at the faded carpet and the dull, dingy staircase. In one of his paws he carried his flute in its case. "This house suits me," he said. He pointed down the hall. "I'll take *that* room."

"A bear!" declared Mr Murgatroyd in disgust. "A bear! Mrs Piper and her twenty children, a man and his mermaid wife, a wispy little woman, peg-legged like a pirate ... What sort of tenants are these?" A slow smile spread over his face. "Think how they'll fight!" he muttered. "All I've got to do is wait, and then they'll fight each other out into the street again, and then I'll get new tenants. I don't fancy this group, even if they are all paying too much."

All the quietness of Mr Murgatroyd's house had gone. Up and down the stairs the children ran and slid and shouted and laughed. The little wispy woman's sloppy-slippered foot went *flup-flup-flup* and her wooden one went *clunk-clunk-clunk*. The bear played strange bear tunes on his flute, and in the bathroom the mermaid wife made a sound like a musical gurgling, and sometimes she sang weird, watery songs and splashed water everywhere with her tail.

"Just wait! Just wait!" Mr Murgatroyd muttered. "They'll be fighting soon."

But this was not all. Miss Wispy brought home potted plants and had a window-box put up outside her window, and planted it with parsley, radishes and petunias. *Flup-clunk, flup-clunk* she went as she tended her garden every day, watering and weeding.

Mrs Piper and all her twenty children took up painting and filled the house with pictures of hills and oceans and the wild, leftover bits of the world. Besides, they painted the kitchen door blue and the staircase pink, and they painted bright pictures on the wall all the way up the stairs.

The mermaid wife sat in the bath and gurgled or sang, depending on her mood. Her husband spread crumbs and honey on the windowsill so that the birds and butterflies came from far away to sit and feast in his room.

And a brown bear with a violin came to play duets with the black bear who played the flute. Mr Murgatroyd did not know what to do.

"They'll be fighting," he promised himself. "Soon they'll be fighting!"

But they *didn't* fight: the mermaid and her husband loved the pink staircase and the bright pictures on the wall. The twenty children laughed to see the bird and butterflies flying around in the house and stood quietly to listen to the bear's flute. The bear loved to play the flute accompaniments to the mermaid's songs, and Miss Wispy made sandwiches for everyone.

At night Mr Murgatroyd would creep into

the hall and listen. "They're all in the mermaid's room singing," he'd guess. "Or is it Mrs Piper's? Anyhow, they're all happy … *When* is the fighting going to begin?" He wandered up and down peering at the pictures on the wall. "They're just pictures of hills," he said. "What's so special about *them?*" He blinked and turned his back on them.

But one day Mr Murgatroyd woke up and there was a new feeling in the house. There was noise and moving as usual, but it felt and sounded very purposeful, as if all the moving was in the same direction. It was like the rustle of a river or the roaring of the sea. Mr Murgatroyd looked out into the hall and saw it was filled with bags and bundles. The bear's flute lay there in its case. Miss Wispy's best potted plant was there. The mermaid's wheelbarrow was parked by the door.

"What's going on?" asked Mr Murgatroyd.

Mrs Piper, who was coming down the pink staircase, her arms full of clothes and toys and satchels and books, smiled at him. "Oh, Mr Murgatroyd – we're all moving out. We've grown tired of paying too much and we get on so well together we thought we'd be up and off and find some other living-place. It may be a forest, it may be a hill, it may be a cave by the sea – where we can sing and watch the birds fly and the plants grow, or listen to the music of flute and fiddle."

Mr Murgatroyd blinked at her and went back into his small, ugly room.

"Good!" he said. "*That's* good. I'm getting rid of all of them at once. Now I'll get some *ordinary* tenants – ones I don't have to worry about. I wonder where they're going?"

He squinted through the keyhole and saw his strange household milling and moiling in the hall, rather like a hive of bees about to swarm. Then the bear struck up a tune on his flute. They all hoisted their baggage and off they went – Mrs Piper and her twenty children, all with their bright bundles, the man wheeling his mermaid wife in the squeaky wheelbarrow, the peg-legged Miss Wispy carrying a potted plant almost as tall as she was, and the bear fluting a silver march for them to walk to.

Mr Murgatroyd saw them go. "Good!" he

said. "Good!" But he didn't feel as happy as he expected he would.

Mr Murgatroyd began to prowl over his newly emptied house. It was very, very quiet, but still bright with pictures on the walls and the pink staircase. Ivy had grown all over the walls of Miss Wispy's room. The bath was filled with sand and shells and seaweed. Only the bear's room was just the same as it had ever been.

Suddenly Mr Murgatroyd knew that the house was his no longer. His strange tenants had made it their own, then left it behind them.

Mr Murgatroyd didn't want to stay there any more. Why, I'll miss them! he thought, amazed and frightened at the thought of missing anyone. He ran to his paintpot and painted a new sign and stuck it up outside his house.

ROOMS TO LET – FREE

Then he packed his toothbrush and nightshirt in a bright bundle of his own and ran out of the door. Far, far up the road he saw the procession of his tenants skipping along, looking like butterflies in the sunlight.

"Wait!" called Mr Murgatroyd. "Wait for *me!*"

SHOCK FOREST

The Carmodys found the red gate easily when they knew exactly what it was they had to look for.

"Just over the hill, and we'll be there," said Eddie's mother.

"Our own forest!" said Eddie. "A whole forest! All ours!"

They had inherited something out of a fairy tale. "A whole forest," Eddie said again.

"I'm *soooo* sick of hearing you say that," groaned Tara. "Does this look like the gate of a grand old house? Be real!"

It was true Eddie had imagined large iron gates and stone gateposts, rather than this wooden gate sagging on rusty hinges. An avenue of tall gum trees curved away behind the gate. The hillside, running up on the right of the gum trees and running down on the left, was covered in a pelt of hairy brown grass and tussocks.

"Open the gate, Tara," said their father. "That'll give you something to do besides grumbling."

Tara scrambled out and stamped towards

the gate, muttering all the way. She had not wanted to leave the city, or her good friends, the shops and the swimming pool. She hated the thought of Shock Forest, and was frightened that her parents might decide, now that her father was out of work, to live there for ever.

"Five hours grumbling! She might get into *The Guinness Book of Records*," said Eddie.

The car rocked forward, struggling and staggering over hidden ruts in the drive.

"Oh, wow!" cried Tara savagely, delighted to think things might be turning out just as badly as she had always said they would.

The two lines of gum trees came to an end, and the Carmodys bounced up to the top of the slope. Shock Forest lay before them.

The hillside facing them was as brown as all other hills in that part of the world, and almost as empty. Almost – but not quite! Rising among the grass and tussocks were hundreds of blackened fingers, all pointing darkly at the sky.

"A shock!" said Eddie. "A real shock!"

"But your father must have known," said

his mother.

"I don't think he did. Well, he never came here," said Mr Carmody. "And Mr Caxton never said anything." Mr Caxton was a young lawyer.

"We have inherited a forest!" cried Tara, copying her father's astonished cry of a fortnight earlier. "And – hey, Dad – can that dump over there possibly be the great Shock mansion?"

"Well, it's big enough," said Mr Carmody defensively.

The house sprawled out a hundred metres to their right. It was big, but battered, too, and badly in need of a coat of paint. All the windows looking back towards the forest seemed to be boarded over.

"Oh, well," said Mrs Carmody, "a house is a house. And I'm longing for a cup of tea."

"I thought there would be lawns and gardens," sighed Eddie, his dreams of grandeur fading. Tussocks marched up to the house and rubbed their tawny heads against its walls.

"The rose gardens and fountains will be on

the *other* side," declared Tara, sounding more and more entertained as things grew worse and worse. "Just like Shock Forest was going to be on the *other* side of the hill."

"Oh, shut up, Tara!" said Mr Carmody wearily. "Give us a break!"

They drove up to the house and stopped at the door.

Mr Carmody turned the large iron key in the lock. The door swung open at once, whining, as if it were afraid of being knocked on, and the Carmodys found themselves in a hall with hooks for coats, and a straight-backed chair with carving on its back and arms. The carpet rustled under their feet. It was covered in dry leaves.

"They must have drifted in under the door," said Mrs Carmody.

"But where did they drift from?" asked Mr Carmody. "There isn't a tree in sight. And look! Ashes!"

"We'll sweep it all up tomorrow," said Mrs Carmody. "My tongue's hanging out for a cup of tea right now."

They came into a big room with a fireplace and wide, soft chairs, worn but homely. A huge mantlepiece running above the fireplace was crowded with photographs. In the centre was a picture of a laughing old man, old-fashioned but handsome, and, beside that, the picture of a woman with thick, streaky hair sitting in the very carved chair they had seen in the hall. At one end of the mantlepiece was a stuffed bird ... a hawk with sad, dusty wings outspread, casting a narrow shadow across the photographs.

"Let's unpack," said Mr Carmody.

"Unpack! We're not staying!" cried Tara. And Eddie realized that she had cheered up a few minutes earlier because she had imagined that, now her parents had seen what Shock Forest was actually like, they would naturally go straight home again. Yet, in the end, even Tara was curious about the house, and helped carry things into the kitchen so she could explore without appearing too interested. Eddie followed her.

It was what people call a farmhouse kitchen, which meant it was as big as most people's dining rooms. An old spade and a worn broom leaned against each other at the back door, and the windows on either side of the door were boarded over. In spite of this, Eddie had the curious feeling that someone was watching them. In a horror film, Great Aunt Isobel would turn out to be sneaking silently up and down secret stairs and spying through hidden peepholes into the lives of other people. As he thought this, Eddie noticed a small hole in the red-boarded wall behind the door – the perfect peephole for a phantom aunt.

That night Eddie lay awake in darkness. The window of his room was boarded over just as the kitchen window had been. But what had Great Aunt Isobel been trying to keep in? Or what had she been trying to keep out? There, in the partly blinded house, Eddie listened to a silence which was not quite silent. Eddie thought he might be hearing the hills breathing, for the sound, if it was a sound, was faint, but vast, too ... vast, distant and lonely. In the end it sang him to sleep. Yet, once his eyes closed, his eyelids immediately grew transparent, and he looked up through them at an angry red light seething on the ceiling over his bed. And then, as he watched in terror through these glass eyelids, a voice whispered and wept in his ear.

"Burned! It burned," said the voice. "It's still burning! And I'm burning, too. I lost him. And I lost my way."

Suddenly, Eddie's eyelids were no longer glassy; he was awake and knew he had been dreaming. Yet his dream felt as if it had been more than a dream. It felt like a vision. Thin, straight lines of golden light shone through cracks in the boards on the other side of the glass. Outside, on the brown hillside, it was morning.

After breakfast the Carmodys wandered down the slope behind the house, up the opposite hillside and into the burned forest. Tara stalked on ahead, occasionally shouting over her shoulder.

"You could keep a horse here," was one of the things she suddenly called. Years ago she had longed for a horse, but they had never had room for one.

"You know, it's beautiful – in its own way, that is," said Mr Carmody, sounding puzzled by this observation.

Tara spun round, walking backwards in amazement.

"Beautiful?" she cried. "Get real, Dad! Those Shocks burned their forest. And they didn't even make a good farm out of what was left."

"It's certainly not great farming land," agreed Mrs Carmody, who had lived on a farm herself when she was a child, but on a green, dairy farm, as easy to run as a farm could ever be.

"I don't think they tried very hard," said Mr Carmody. "They were always struggling. Independent, though! Toby was not only dead but buried before she ever let any of us know. She was ... well ... not hostile exactly, just aloof."

"That's right! Blame the woman!" exclaimed Tara.

"No, it's nothing to do with blame," said Mr

Carmody. "Everyone says she adored old Toby. But they kept to themselves ... and to Shock Forest, of course."

"What's that – that cage over there?" Eddie asked, pointing.

He was watching Tara who had come to a standstill beside a pen of some kind, fenced around with spiky iron railings.

"It's a – a grave," said Mrs Carmody. She hesitated, then walked towards it.

"Guess whose?" asked Tara.

Inside the spikes of iron was a space about as big as a double bed. One grave was covered by a long, flat stone and the other by a mound of earth. Both graves were covered with leaves.

"Why didn't they just pack up and move to the city when they got older?" asked Mrs Carmody. "It makes me sad, thinking of them struggling out here, looking at burned trees day after day."

"They didn't look at them," said Tara. "The windows that overlook the forest are all boarded up."

From the top of the long slope they could see sunburnt fingers of land stretching out, then folding in between one another. In the distance they could make out a slot of misty ocean.

"There's forest all the way to the sea," said Eddie.

"Native bush," Tara corrected him. "Not high, though."

"Gorse," said their father. "That's gorse and broom! People cleared the native trees, and the gorse and broom just cheered and took over. Mad colonists!"

"Why would anyone bring gorse to a new land?" Mrs Carmody asked. "Well, let's be glad that we don't have that particular trouble on this hill."

"Why don't we have gorse when everyone else does?" asked Eddie.

"Good question!" Mr Carmody looked from side to side, studying the different greens of the distant slopes, frowning. "I suppose the Shocks must have sprayed it. Or grubbed it out."

But thinking of the neglected hillside they

had just climbed, it was hard to believe that Great Aunt Isobel Shock had cared whether gorse grew there or not.

"I thought I could hear the sea last night," said Mrs Carmody at last, looking across to the sea, "but now it looks too far away to be heard."

"I heard it, too," said Tara, "but perhaps it was only the wind."

"Yes … though nothing rattled," Mrs Carmody pointed out. "Things rattle in an old house."

"Mysteries! Mysteries!" Mr Carmody sighed. "No gorse! No rattling! Now listen – especially you, Tara! I know you're longing to get back to the city but I want to think things over, talk to a few people around here and find out just what possibilities there are."

"I could feel this coming," said Tara. "Find someone who has a burnt-tree collection, and sell it. That's my advice."

All the same she didn't sound as angry as she had yesterday. Eddie thought she sounded puzzled and even, if it were possible, a little scared.

Once again Eddie lay in bed, uncertain if

his eyes were open or if he were looking through glass eyelids once more. Once again he was seeing that reddish flicker move restlessly over the walls and ceilings. And yet, if he turned his head sideways, there on the floor were his jeans and jacket, collapsed into a heap that still, somehow, had his own shape pressed into it ... too real to be part of any dream. Perhaps it was not him but the air of his room that was dreaming – dreaming of fire.

Eddie corrected himself. Air could not dream. The white walls must be reflecting fire from somewhere else. Scrambling out of bed, he pressed his eye to the glass, lined it up with a crack and peered outside.

The hillside behind the house was burning. He could make out the shapes of great trees, their arms flung up in horror at what was happening to them. Their fingers burned, their skin burned, and now Eddie could hear once again that curious, soft roar that seemed to come, not merely from the other side of the glass, but from spaces inside the house as well –

spaces that were stealing heat in order to set the ghostly fires roaring once more. That's why (even as he listened to the huge breath of the flames and shared the hillside's terrible, reviving memory) Eddie was shivering. Outside, burning trees lashed from side to side, as if in agony.

Eddie knew he must see all there was to see. He left the window, went downstairs, crossed the big room (dry leaves once more crackling under his feet) and went through the kitchen to the back door. It stood slightly open. Something moved on the other side of it, black against the trembling red.

A hand fell on his shoulder. Eddie thought he would die of fear. He turned with his cry still caught in his throat, and found himself staring into Tara's face.

She put a finger across her lips, as Eddie waved a shaking hand towards the door, then snatched up a broom from where it leaned against the kitchen bench and pushed the door open.

Great Uncle Toby Shock gazed back at them. He looked exactly like the young man in the photograph on the mantlepiece but he was burning like a tree – burning without actually being consumed, and giving off chill not warmth. His lips flickered as if they were made of flame, and when words came, they did so in the breathless, roaring voice of the fire. Their great-uncle was asking them a riddle.

> *"We went into the green and the green became red,*
> *But inside the red I have hidden the green.*
> *Give the green to the black where the green burned and bled.*
> *What-will-be will grow out of time-that-has-been."*

Tara suddenly thrust the broom against the door, slamming it shut. The painted wood twitched and shivered as if it, too, could feel the cold.

The voice on the other side of the door sang a second riddle.

> *"Over the fire, there flies a bird,*
> *And on the bird is a hook of horn,*
> *And in the hook there lies a key.*
> *Unlock the red and loose the green."*

And suddenly it was over. The door stopped quivering. The kitchen was filled with an ordinary darkness.

"Why does this ghost have to ask riddles?" asked Eddie, his voice shaking.

"We *hear* riddles," Tara replied. "It's because they don't match up with us. Anyhow, that second riddle's easy."

Eddie followed her into the sitting room. Tara reached up and ran her fingers along the beak of the stuffed hawk. Something clinked as it tumbled away across the hearth and into the leaves on the carpet. She picked it up.

"A key!" she said. "To unlock the red. But how can you unlock a fire?"

"I don't know," said Eddie. He suddenly felt limp and heavy as if he must sleep. The riddles were working in him. He must sleep, and perhaps, in sleep, he might even dream the answers.

"Where do these leaves come from?" cried Mrs Carmody next morning. "Leaves and ashes! Look at them!" She looked cross, but a little frightened, too. "I swept this hearth yesterday, but it's messed up again."

In the kitchen Eddie suddenly remembered the little hole he had seen watching him the first time he walked into the kitchen. Now he looked closely, he could see it was a keyhole in a door without a handle, flush with the wall and also painted red.

"I've found a door," he called to Tara.

Tara had fastened the key to her charm bracelet. By holding her left hand close to the wall, and jiggling the key with her right, she unlocked the door.

"What have you found there?" asked Mrs Carmody. "Oh, look! A spice cupboard! And spice jars!"

"Cloves and nutmegs!" said Tara. But she sounded doubtful. She pulled the cork from one of the jars. "They're not green. They're all shrivelled up."

"It says 'Kanuka' on this jar," said Eddie, reading the labels. "Kanuka, ngaio, cabbage tree ..."

"Seeds," said Mrs Carmody with sudden

interest. "Tree seeds. Get planting, kids. There's a big future in forestry."

"It's not as funny as you might think," said Mr Carmody. "There is a future in forestry."

"Those seeds are probably too old to grow," Mrs Carmody said.

But Eddie was reaching for the spade behind the door. It seemed to leap into his hand.

"I'll plant them," he offered. Tara watched him, frowning.

"I'll help," she said. Eddie saw his father and mother look at her in amazement. But Tara didn't notice. She was thinking of something else. "*Out of the red*," she muttered to Eddie, "that red cupboard, for example, we'll *bring the green* ... that's the seeds ... and then we will see what there is to be seen. I read somewhere that seeds which have been buried in pyramids for three thousand years will still grow."

Besides the spade, they found a small garden fork and a hoe propped against the wall just outside the back door. Together they began to dig on either side of the brick path that stretched out to the rusting clothes line. No one had dug there for a long time: the ground was hard and unwilling. Yet, finally, they finished digging it over, first with the spade, then with the fork, pulling out the long roots of twitch grass, smashing the lumps of soil with the back of the fork, and crumbling the smaller lumps with the hoe. As they worked, the seeds sat in a jar soaking in rainwater from the tank. That evening they planted them in two long, straight rows, one on either side of the path.

Later that night Eddie woke to hear, not a roar but a whisper, and the scratch of fingers at his window. Through last night's crack he saw the fire once more, but fainter and more distant. Something dark swayed backwards and forwards on the other side of the boards, but he couldn't make out what it was.

His door opened. Tara stood there, beckoning him to follow her downstairs and through the open kitchen door.

Trees again, but growing now, not

burning. These trees reached forward to brush their faces with new bending twigs and young leaves. These trees welcomed them.

"Our seeds!" exclaimed Tara. "These are our seeds. That's a cabbage tree, and I remember pushing cabbage-tree seeds into the dirt just there, I told them to grow, and they are growing. That's the tree my seed grew into."

Together they stepped into a future forest. The air was softened with fine rain ... nothing much more than a mist ... smelling of wet leaves and soil and ferns. The trees went on and on and on.

"But we didn't plant all these," Tara said, sounding puzzled.

"We will, though," Eddie cried, sure he was right. "We'll plant more tomorrow. Shock Forest is starting all over again."

Red light flowed towards them. They had come to a boundary between the green, growing forest of the future and the burning trees of the past. And there, on the boundary between growing and burning, sitting in her large, carved chair, was Great Aunt Isobel Shock. Time was her sitting room now. The stiff, springy hair that stood out around her face blazed angrily, yet Isobel Shock was shivering.

"I burned them!" she cried. Her teeth chattered, chopping the words short. "They hate me. They hold me."

"Who?" asked Eddie, amazed.

"The trees hate me," she said. Tears, reflecting the flames, ran down her cheeks in smouldering lines.

"We were going to make a farm. We were going to live happily ever after. Why not? I know the Maori people said it was *tapu* and that no one should touch it, but land is meant to be used. And then – and then the forest *bewitched* Toby. He'd walk among the trees, and come back happy. *I* wouldn't walk with him. Why should I learn to love the trees? That land they were growing on was meant to be our farm. But, at last, one dry, summer day when Toby was in town and the wind was blowing towards the sea, I did go into the forest ... went into the forest carrying paper and petrol and matches. The trees whispered to me, but I wouldn't listen. Not me! I crumpled the paper ... piled the sticks ... poured the petrol. 'Tssst!' went the match. The forest burned and burned and burned. It turned to ashes. Toby drove up, and, as we stood side by side watching it burn, I felt something inside Toby turning to ashes, too."

She fell silent.

"What happened after that?" asked Eddie.

"After that?" said Great Aunt Isobel. "Nothing happened except that we grew older. The forest is still burning. Our farm never thrived. Toby died."

Her voice was growing fainter.

"I can hear his voice calling my name, but the forest is holding me."

Then, suddenly, she began to burn all over, twitching and twisting in the embrace of the fire.

Tara caught Eddie's arm and they ran down the hill, under their cool trees, and back to the house again.

At breakfast, Mr Carmody said he was going to talk to the man at the shop.

"I'll come, too," said Tara. "I'll open the gate."

"Now, *there's* a change," said Mr Carmody. Tara grinned.

"I've had gate-opening experience," she said. "You might wreck the delicate hinges."

THE BRIDGE BUILDER

My father was a bridge builder. When I was small, bridges brought us bread and books, Christmas crackers and coloured pencils – one-span bridges over creeks, two-span bridges over streams, three-span bridges over wide rivers. Bridges sprang from my father's dreams threading roads together – girder bridges, arched bridges, suspension bridges, bridges of wood, bridges of iron or concrete. His bridges became visible parts of the world's hidden skeleton. When we went out on picnics it was along roads held together by my father's works. As we crossed rivers and ravines we heard each bridge singing in its own private language. We could hear the melody, but my father was the only one who understood the words.

There were three of us when I was small: Philippa, the oldest, Simon in the middle, and me, Merlin, the youngest, the one with the magician's name. We played where bridges were being born, running around piles of sand and shingle, bags of cement and bars of reinforced steel. Concrete mixers would turn, winches would wind, piles would be driven and decking cast. Slowly, as we watched and played, a bridge would appear and people could cross over.

For years my father built bridges where people said they wanted them, while his children stretched up and out in three different directions. Philippa became a doctor and Simon an electrical engineer, but I became a traveller, following the roads of the world and crossing the world's bridges as I came to them.

My father, however, remained a bridge builder. When my mother died and we children were grown up and gone, and there was no more need for balloons and books or Christmas crackers and coloured pencils, his stored powers were set free and he began to build the bridges he saw in his dreams.

The first of his new bridges had remarkable handrails of black iron lace. But this was not enough for my father. He collected a hundred orb-web spiders and set them loose in the crevices and curlicues of the iron. Within the lace of the bridge, these spiders spun their own lace, and after a night of rain or dew the whole bridge glittered black and silver.

People were enchanted with the unexpectedness of it. Now, as they crossed over, they became part of a work of art. But the same people certainly thought my father strange when he built another bridge of horsehair and vines so that rabbits, and even mice, could cross the river with dry feet and tails. He's gone all funny, they said, turning their mouths down.

However, my father had only just begun. Over a river that wound through a grove of silver birch trees he wove a bridge of golden wires, a great cage filled with brilliant, singing birds; and in a dull, tired town he made an aquarium bridge whose glass balustrades and parapets were streaked scarlet and gold by the fish that darted inside them. People began to go out of their way to cross my father's bridges.

Building surprising bridges was one thing,

but soon my father took it into his head to build bridges in unexpected places. He gave up building them where people were known to be going and built them where people might happen to find themselves. Somewhere, far from any road, sliding through brush and ferns to reach a remote stretch of river, you might find one of my father's bridges: perhaps a strong one built to last a thousand years, perhaps a frail one made of bamboo canes, peacock feathers and violin strings. A bridge like this would soon fall to pieces sending its peacock feathers down the river like messages, sounding a single twangling note among the listening hills. Mystery became a part of crossing over by my father's bridges.

In some ways it seemed as if his ideas about what a bridge should be were changing. His next bridge, made of silver thread and mother of pearl, was only to be crossed at midnight on a moonlight night. So, crossing over changed, too. Those who crossed over from one bank to another on this bridge, crossed also from one day to another, crossing time as well as the spaces under the piers. It was his first time-bridge, but later there was to be another, a bridge set with clocks chiming perpetually the hours and half hours in other parts of the world. And in all the world this was the only bridge that needed to be wound up with a master key every eight days.

Wherever my father saw a promising space he thought of ways in which it could be crossed, and yet for all that he loved spaces. In the city he climbed like a spider, stringing blue suspension bridges between skyscrapers and lower blocks – air bridges, he called them. Looking up at them from the street they became invisible. When crossing over on them, you felt you were suspended in nothing, or were maybe set in crystal, a true inhabitant of the sky. Lying down, looking through the blue web that held you, you could see the world turning below. But if you chose to lie on your back all the architecture of the air would open up to you.

However, not many people bothered to stare upwards like that. Only the true travellers were fascinated to realize that the space they carelessly passed through was not empty, but crowded with its own invisible constructions.

"Who wants a bridge like that, anyway?" some people asked sourly.

"Anyone. Someone!" my father answered. "There are no rules for crossing over."

But a lot of people disagreed with this idea of my father's. Such people thought bridges were designed specially for cars, mere pieces of road stuck up on legs of iron or concrete, whereas my father thought bridges were the connections that would hold everything together. Bridges gone, perhaps the whole world would fall apart, like a quartered orange. The journey on the left bank of the river (according to my father) was quite different from the journey on the right. The man on the right bank of the ravine – was he truly the same man when he crossed on to the left? My father thought he might not be, and his bridges seemed like the steps of a dance which would enable the man with a bit of left-hand spin on him to spin in the opposite direction. This world (my father thought) was playing a great game called "change", and his part in the game was called "crossing over".

It was upsetting for those people who wanted to stick to the road to know that some people used my father's hidden bridges. They wanted everyone to cross by exactly the same bridges that *they* used, and they hated the thought that, somewhere over the river they were crossing, there might be another strange and lovely bridge they were unaware of.

However, no one could cross all my father's bridges. No one can cross over in every way. Some people became angry when they realized this and, because they could not cross over on every bridge there was, they started insisting that there should be no more bridge building. Some of these people were very powerful – so powerful, indeed, that they passed laws forbidding my father to build any bridge unless ordered to do so by a government or by some county council. They might as well have passed a law saying that the tide was only allowed to come in and out by government decree, because by now my father's bridge building had become a force beyond the rule of law. He built another bridge, a secret one, which was not discovered until he had finished it, this time over a volcano. Men, women and children who crossed over could look down into the glowing heart of the volcano, could watch it simmer and seethe and smoulder. And when the winds blew, or when the great fumes of hot air billowed up like dragon's breath, the harps played fiery music.

"The bridge will melt when the volcano erupts," people said to each other, alarmed and fascinated by these anthems of fire.

"But none of my bridges are intended to last for ever," my father muttered to himself, loading his derrick and winch on to the back of his truck and driving off in another direction. It was just as well he kept on the move. Powerful enemies pursued him.

"Bridges are merely bits of the road with special problems," they told one another, and sent soldiers out to trap my father, to arrest him, to put an end to his bridge building. Of course, they couldn't catch him. They would think they had him cornered and, behold, he would build a bridge and escape – a bridge that collapsed behind him as if it had been made of playing cards, or a bridge that unexpectedly turned into a boat, carrying his astonished pursuers away down some swift river.

Just about then, as it happened, my travelling took me on my first circle around the world, and I wound up back where I had started from. My brother, the electrical engineer, and my sister, the doctor, came to see me camping under a bridge that my father had built when I was only three years old.

"Perhaps you can do something about him," Philippa cried. "He won't listen to us."

"Don't you care?" asked Simon. "It's a real embarrassment. It's time he was stopped before he brings terrible trouble upon himself."

They looked at me – shaggy and silent, with almost nothing to say to them – in amazement.

I gave them the only answer I could.

"What is there for a bridge builder to build, if he isn't allowed to build bridges?" I asked them. Dust from the world's roads made my voice husky, even in my own ears.

"He can be a retired bridge builder," Simon replied. "But I can see that you're going to waste time asking riddles. You don't care that your old father is involved in illegal bridge-building." And he went away. He had forgotten the weekend picnics in the sunshine, and the derrick, high as a ladder, leading to the stars.

"And what have you become, Merlin?" Philippa asked me. "What are you now, after all your journeys?"

"I'm a traveller as I always have been," I replied.

"You are a vagabond," she answered scornfully. "A vagabond with a magician's name, but no magic!"

Then she went away, too, in her expensive car. I did not tell her, but I did have a little bit of magic – a single magical word, half-learned, half-invented. I could see that my father might need help, even a vagabond's help, even the help of a single magic word. I set off to find him.

It was easy for me, a seasoned traveller, to fall in with my father. I just walked along, until I came to a river that sang his name, and then I followed that river up over slippery stones and waterfalls, through bright green tangles of cress and monkey musk. Sure enough, there was my father building a bridge by bending two tall trees over the water and plaiting the branches into steps. This bridge would, in time, grow leafy handrails filled with birds' nests, a crossing place for deer and possums.

"Hello!" said my father. "Hello, Merlin. I've just boiled the billy. Care for a cup of tea?"

"Love one!" I said. "There's nothing quite like a cup of billy-tea." So we sat down in a patch of sunlight and drank our tea.

"They're catching up with me, you know," my father said sadly. "There are police and soldiers looking all the time. Helicopters, too! I can go on escaping, of course, but I'm not sure if

I can be bothered. I'm getting pretty bored with it all. Besides," he went on, lowering his voice as if the green shadows might overhear him, "I'm not sure that building bridges is enough any longer. I feel I must become more involved, to cross over myself in some way. But how does a bridge builder learn to cross over when he's on both sides of the river to begin with?"

"I might be able to help," I said.

My father looked up from under the brim of his working hat. He was a weatherbeaten man, fingernails cracked by many years of bridge building. Sitting there, a cup of billy-tea between his hands, he looked like a tree, he looked like a rock.

"I'm not sure you can," he answered. "I must be *more* of a bridge builder not less of one, if you understand me."

"Choosy, aren't you?" I said, smiling, and he smiled back.

"I suppose you think you know what I'd like most," he went on.

"I think I do!" I replied. "I've crossed a lot

of bridges myself one way and another, because I'm a travelling man, and I've learned a lot on the banks of many rivers."

"And you've a magical name," my father reminded me eagerly. "I said, when you were born, this one is going to be the magician of the family!"

"I'm not a magician," I replied, "but there is one word I know ... a word of release and remaking. It allows things to become their true selves." My father was silent for a moment, nodding slowly, eyes gleaming under wrinkled lids.

"Don't you think things are really what they seem to be?" he asked me.

"I think people are all, more or less, creatures of two sides with a chasm in between, so to speak. My magic word merely closes the chasm."

"A big job for one word," said my father.

"Well, it's a very good word," I said. I didn't tell him I had invented half of it myself. "It's a sort of bridge," I told him.

All the time we talked, we had felt the

movement of men, not very close, not very far, as the forest carried news of my father's pursuers. Now we heard a sudden sharp cry – and another – and another. Men shouted in desperate voices.

"It's the soldiers," my father said, leaping to his feet. "They've been hunting me all day, though the forest is on my side and hides me away. But something's happened. We'd better go and check what's going on. I don't want them to come to harm because of me and my bridge building habits."

We scrambled upstream until the river suddenly started to run more swiftly, narrow and deep. The opposite bank rose up sharply, red with crumbling, rotten rock, green with mosses and pockets of fern. My father struggled to keep up with me. He was old, and besides, he was a bridge builder, not a traveller. Closing my eyes for a moment against the distractions around me, I brought the magic word out of my mind and on to the tip of my tongue – and, then I left it unspoken.

The soldiers were on the opposite bank. They had tried to climb down the cliff on rotten rock but it had broken away at their very toes and there they were, marooned on a crumbling ledge – three of them – weighted down with guns, ammunition belts and other military paraphernalia. Two of the soldiers were very young, and all three of them were afraid, faces pale, reflecting the green leaves greenly.

Below them the rocks rose out of the water. Just at this point the river became a dragon's mouth, full of black teeth, hissing and roaring, sending up a faint smoke of silver spray.

It was obvious that the soldiers needed a bridge.

My father stared at them, and they stared at him like men confounded. But he was a bridge-builder before he was anybody's friend or enemy, before he was anybody's father.

"That word?" he asked me. "You have it there?"

I nodded. I dared not speak, or the word would be said too soon.

"When I step into the water, say it then, Merlin!"

I waited and my father smiled at me, shy and proud and mischievous all at once. He looked up once at the sky, pale blue and far, and then he stepped, one foot on land, one in the water, towards the opposite bank. I spoke the word.

My father changed before my eyes. He became a bridge as he had known he would. As for the word – it whispered over the restless surface of the river and rang lightly on the red, rotten rock. But my father had taken its magic out of it. No one else was altered.

The curious thing was that my father, who had made so many strange and beautiful bridges, was a very ordinary-looking bridge himself – a single-span bridge built of stone over an arch of stone, springing upwards at an odd angle, vanishing into the cliff at the very feet of the terrified soldiers. He looked as if he had always been there, as if he would be there for ever, silver moss on his handrails, on his abutments, even on his deck. Certainly he was the quietest bridge I had ever crossed as I went over to help the soldiers down. There was no way forward through the cliff. Still, perhaps the job of some rare bridges is to cross over only briefly and then bring us back to the place we started from.

We came back together, the three soldiers and I, and I'm sure we were all different men on the right bank from the men we had been on the left.

Our feet made no sound on the silver moss.

"They can say what they like about that old man," cried the older soldier all of a sudden, "but I was never so pleased to see a bridge in all my life. It just shows there are good reasons for having bridges in unexpected places."

Together we scrambled downstream, and at last, back on to the road.

"But who's going to build the bridges now, then?" asked one of the young soldiers. "Look! You were with him. Are you a bridge-builder, too?"

They knew now. They knew that unexpected bridges would be needed.

But someone else will have to build them. I am not a bridge-builder. I am a traveller. I set out travelling, after that, crossing, one by one, all the bridges my father had built ... the picnic-bridges of childhood, the wooden ones, the steel ones, the stone and the concrete. I crossed the blue bridges of the air and those that seemed to be woven of vines and flowers. I crossed the silver-thread and mother-of-pearl bridge one moonlit midnight. I looked down into the melting heart of the world and saw my reflection in a bubble of fire while the harps sang and sighed and snarled around me with the very voice of the volcano.

Some day someone, perhaps my own child, may say that word of mine back to me – that word I said to my father – but I won't turn into a bridge. I shall become a journey winding over hills, across cities, along seashores and through shrouded forests, crossing my father's bridges and the bridges of other men, as well as all the infinitely divided roads and splintered pathways that lie between them.

The TRAVELLING BOY
AND THE
STAY-AT-HOME BIRD

Sam lived with his anxious Great-Aunt Angela in a house with high hedges and a closed gate. When she was behind her high hedge with the gate slammed shut Great-Aunt Angela was happy. Jaunts, junkets and journeys worried her to bits, but a closed gate soothed her, smoothed her, made her feel serene. In her little sun-porch she would knit and sew and sing like a spring blackbird and, sometimes, snatch a catnap as well, whereas a journey, even to the shops, made her go all fidgety and fretful. At such times she became a very difficult great-aunt for a boy like Sam.

Sam had eyes halfway between sky-blue and sea-green. You never saw a boy with such a look of distance about him. There were a thousand journeys locked up inside him waiting to get out.

"Go here! Go there! Walk! Run! Skate! Sail! Fly!" said the voices in his head. "Get there somehow!" But Sam was not allowed to do any of these things. The gate was always shut, and he was forbidden to go into the dirty, dangerous world outside.

Sometimes, however, Great-Aunt Angela, though rather short-sighted herself, saw Sam's blue-green look of distance and overheard the echo of the voices inside his head.

"I suppose he needs some lively company," she thought. "I'm not very fond of animals, but perhaps a good, clean pet of some kind …" and, very bravely, she put on her boots and her good going-out coat, took her shopping trundler and called Sam. Then they set out together to visit the Paramount Pet Shop, which was all of two corners away. They crossed the street when the traffic lights told them to cross and Sam could see four roads, all going in different directions. One road led to the sea, another to the mountains, one pointed to the South Pole and another to the Equator. He was surrounded by possible journeys and all the roads seemed to be saying, "Take me! Take me!"

Men had made a hole in the street and its black mouth hissed, "Down here! Down here!" as Sam went by. He looked up and the sky was filled with travellers … a Piper Cherokee plane from the aero club, a couple of ducks in search of the river, and a whole crowd of sparrows, flying in every direction. "Up and away! Up and away!" they cried, but only Sam could hear them.

Great-Aunt Angela's own ears were too full of rattling footsteps, roaring cars, and raging trucks to hear the voices of possible journeys crying out to her.

When they got to the Paramount Pet Shop there were pets of all kinds to choose from – dogs, cats, guinea pigs, rabbits – but Great-Aunt Angela did not want anything that would track in dirt on its paws, or have babies.

"What about a bird?' said the pet shop man, a very secret-looking man, unusual to find behind a public place like a shop counter. "Their cages are very easy to clean. Sam could learn to do that for himself, couldn't you, Sam?"

"I don't want anything that has to live in a cage," Sam said. "I don't like cages."

When the pet shop man heard this he gave

Sam a very careful glance, and Sam stared back, and saw at once that the pet shop man was full of journeys too, but that his journeys had all been taken. He wore them openly on his face, which was lined like a map with the tracery of a thousand explorations.

"Why, I think I have just the pet for you, Sam," he said at last. "It's out the back because it's rather large."

"I can't afford much!" cried Great-Aunt Angela, anxious immediately. "And we don't have much room."

"Oh, they're very cheap, these particular pets," the pet shop man assured her. "They're very hard to place because you've got to wait until the right customer comes along." Then he went out into the back of the shop and returned a moment later with a bird following him ... a tall bird, rather like a patchwork tea-cosy on long yellow legs, quite tame and looking as if it would be no trouble at all around the house.

"It's very brightly coloured," Great-Aunt Angela said nervously, for bright colours were part of the danger of the world to her.

"Oh, that could change," the pet shop man said. "He'll grow to whatever colour you need him to be. And he'll fit into any space you happen to have in the house. Fitting into available space is this bird's speciality. And he'll grow to the exact size that suits you."

Great-Aunt Angela was delighted to hear this. "I do like him," she decided. "I love his blue eyes. We'll take him shall we, Sam, and we'll call him Norton after my late cousin Norton. He'd got a look in his eyes that reminds me of dear Norton very strongly. You'll like that, won't you, Sam?"

"Yes, thank you, Great-Aunt Angela," Sam replied.

But in his mind Sam called the bird Fernando Eagle, the freest name he could think of, a name for some buccaneer or bold adventurer who also happened to be a bird.

"He's too tame, really," Sam thought. "He's over-tamed, but I'll un-tame him. I'll teach him to fight and fly and to be free, and when he does fly away at last – well, it will be almost as good as flying away myself. It will be a kind of promise to me that some day I'll be free too."

Great-Aunt Angela paid the money, and Sam and she walked home through the rattling, roaring, raging streets while Fernando Eagle stalked after them like a particularly well-behaved dog.

At home, with the gate closed and locked, Great-Aunt Angela gave Sam and Fernando Eagle a slice of bread and jam each.

"He needs worms and wigglies, not bread and jam," Sam cried.

"Oh Sam, don't say such things!" Great-Aunt Angela exclaimed in alarm. "I can't bear to think of worms and wigglies. And look –" she added triumphantly – "he's eaten the bread and jam and he's asking for more." And so he had, and so he was.

"Good bird, Norton!" said Great-Aunt Angela, patting him on the head.

Sam saw he had no time to lose and began his plans for the un-taming of Fernando Eagle immediately.

"He hasn't got a mother to teach him," thought Sam, "so I'll have to be a sort of mother to him."

He tried to make himself as much like Fernando Eagle's mother as he could.

First he cut a bird mask out of cardboard but, when he tried it on, Fernando Eagle looked doubtful. Then he wrapped himself in an old curtain covered in red, white and blue squares, but Fernando Eagle merely sighed and shuffled his feet.

"Feet!" thought Sam and he cut himself big bird feet and stuck them on to the soles of his school shoes with sticky tape. Then he painted his new feet and his old legs (up above sock level) with yellow poster paint, and looked hopefully at Fernando Eagle. But Fernando Eagle sank his head deep into his ruff and clacked his beak in alarm.

"Now!" Sam cried. "Listen! This is how eagles call," and he hopped around the room giving wild, dangerous cries of the sort he thought a free bird ought to give, as it took off into the sky. Such cries had never been heard behind the high hedge before. Out in the sunporch Great-Aunt Angela started as if she had been stung and dropped several stitches. Even so, she was not as frightened as Fernando Eagle who ran behind a chair and cowered there, terrified.

"Sam! Sam!" cried Great-Aunt Angela as she burst into Sam's room. "What a noise! Look at the room! Look at your legs! Look at those scraps of cardboard, look at your feet! Look at your face! Look at poor Norton, he's petrified, poor bird, and no wonder! Clean yourself up at once and then sweep the floor! Goodness gracious, what an example to set an innocent pet barely in the house thirty minutes. He'll think you're some sort of hoodlum or noodlum, Sam."

She went out of the room and Fernando Eagle scuttled after her, anxious for quiet dignified company and more bread and jam. Sam was left to tidy up the mess he'd made. He was disappointed but not discouraged.

"It's a beginning," he thought. "I suppose it is pretty confusing for a bird before he realizes what he's supposed to do. But once he catches on he'll love it. Fancy being able to fly! I wish I could. I'll give him a flying-from-tree-to-tree lesson tomorrow and see how he gets on. I want him to be as free as air … as free as – as a bird …"

In the middle of Great-Aunt Angela's little square of lawn was a small tree, doing its best to be a tree in spite of being barbered and bobbed every spring and autumn. Still, if you really wanted to you could climb up into it and from there you could see almost over the top of the high hedge. However, Sam was not supposed to climb it for fear of falling down and hurting himself.

"Look, Fernando!" cried Sam. "Watch me!" He made himself wings out of a corrugated cardboard carton and an old feather duster and tied them in at his wrists and shoulders. Zooming over the lawn he climbed up into the tree so rapidly that it did almost look as if he were flying. He stood on the topmost branch sweeping his wings up and down, and his wild free cries had a real echo of distance in them. It was as if all the journeys locked up inside him were crying out aloud against the high hedges and the closed gates. But Fernando Eagle shook his head and looked back over his shoulder longingly to Great-Aunt Angela's kitchen.

"Blow!" thought Sam. "He's not getting the idea. If only I had another tree ... one's not enough for a proper tree-to-tree exercise." An idea came to him, and he went into Great-Aunt Angela's tiny tool-shed and brought out her all-aluminium-extendible-collapsible step-ladder and stood it close to the tree. He stuck it all over with pieces of hedge and fallen leaves.

"Look, Fernando!" he said, pointing at the tree. "Tree! Tree! Get it?" Fernando pretended to scratch his ear with one foot while balancing on the other, and Sam was encouraged by this display of skill. He pointed to the step-ladder. "Another tree!" he said slowly and clearly, though he had to admit, secretly, that it did not look very like a tree in spite of all his work. "Another tree! Two trees! Now watch!" Waving his wings gracefully he climbed the step-ladder, stood there beautifully balanced and then leaped from the step-ladder into the top branches of Great-Aunt Angela's tree. He did this supremely well … he really did look as if he were flying. But unfortunately Great-Aunt Agatha chose that moment to look through the kitchen window, just checking up.

"Sam!" she screamed. "Oh Sam! Oh! Come down at once, you inconsiderate boy! What's got into you? Are you trying to drive me to my death?"

"I was teaching Fernando how to fly," Sam began to explain, but it was no use. He was called untidy, dirty and dangerous, the sort of boy who would set a bad example to a pet.

"Fernando doesn't need to fly!" Great-Aunt Angela declared. "He doesn't want to fly. Look, you've made him hide his head under his wing, poor thing. And he's been a model bird all day. I was worried to begin with, he was so brightly coloured he looked a bit raffish, but his feathers are beginning to lose that flashy patchiness and settle down to a nice, quiet grey."

And so they were. Parts of him were about the same colour as Sam's school uniform.

"That show's he's happy!" said Great-Aunt Angela with satisfaction. "So don't upset him."

Sam felt desperate. It seemed to him that if Fernando Eagle couldn't learn to fly, he, Sam, would live for ever behind hedges and closed gates until all his journeys withered and died inside him. "Go here! Go there! Up … up … away … awa-a-ay …" called the voices in his head and he thought Fernando Eagle must hear them too. But he didn't. He ate platefuls of bread and jam and grew neater and more school uniformish day by day – taller, too. Now he was just the same size as Sam himself.

Great-Aunt Angela knitted him a little blue scarf and a blue woolly cap with a white tassel, and fussed over him more and more. It was as if Fernando was the real person in the house and

Sam just some sort of unnecessary ghost who had got in behind the high hedge by accident. One day when Sam and Fernando were on the lawn doing nothing much, Sam flapping his arms in a tired fashion and Fernando looking the other way, Great-Aunt Angela came out of the house in her good going-out coat, pushing her shopping trundler in front of her.

"Norton!" she called. "Norr-ton! I'm going down to the supermarket. You may come with me if you like and push the trundler."

Sam was astounded to hear Fernando Eagle reply in a very ordinary voice, as if he had been talking ever since he was hatched out of the egg, "Yes, Aunt Angela! I'd love to. Does Sam have to come as well?"

"Who's Sam?" the Great-Aunt said. "Some little imaginary friend of yours? Now, Norton, don't become too fanciful. Too much fancy is a dangerous thing for a growing boy."

"I will be careful, Auntie, I promise," answered the foolish bird. "I really will. May I push the trundler all the way to the shops?"

"Of course you may," replied Great-Aunt Angela graciously. "You deserve a little treat. You've eaten up your greens and your bread and jam so well lately."

Sam watched them as they set off down the drive. He felt lonely because, though he had never got on very well with Great-Aunt Angela, she was the only relation he had. But more than that, he felt desperate for Fernando Eagle.

"One last chance!" he thought. "One last chance for him to see that he doesn't have to stay here. He can fly away and be free."

"Fernando!" he called. "It's your last chance. You must fly. You must FLY." He ran down the drive after them and all his imprisoned journeys rose up inside him like leaping flames. "Like this, Fernando!" He held out his arms and the world turned under him. Aunt Angela carefully closed her gate but Sam went up over it and did not come down again. The air took him into itself. He, Sam, was the one to fly.

As if he had been flying for years he rose

up higher than the high hedge and saw the whole street beyond – the traffic lights winking at him and the shops behind the traffic lights. He even thought he could see the pet shop man at the pet shop door.

"Up and away!" said a voice like a bell ringing in his head. He had often heard it before but never so clearly and now he could do what it told him to do. Up and away he went, between the painted roofs and the chimneys, frightening sparrows, scolded by startled starlings. Up and away, over the chimneys now, and suddenly all directions were possible for him.

The city looked at first like a game of noughts-and-crosses being played beneath him, and then like a great clockwork Christmas present, muttering to itself while lights flashed on and off.

"Up and away!" said the voice like a bell, and a new silvery voice whispered,

"The sea! The sea!"

"Are you surprised?" asked a third voice, but not in his head. This one came from beside

91

him, and there was the pet shop man flying too. "I saw your aunt and Norton trembling together by the traffic lights so I thought you must be up here somewhere."

Sam thought of Norton and felt sad for the stay-at-home bird. "I wanted him to be Fernando Eagle," he said.

"Fernando Eagle never existed," replied the pet shop man.

"Believe me, you were the eagle of your Great-Aunt's house. There was no eagle space for a bird to fit into. But there was a Norton space ... a grey bread-and-jam-trundler-pushing space ... and he fitted in there exactly. He will be very happy and so will your Great-Aunt. Look! There they go!"

Far below like grey ants, Great-Aunt Angela and Norton crawled back towards the front gate and locked it behind them, shutting out the dangerous clockwork city.

"The sea! The sea!" insisted the silver voice and Sam saw that he was indeed set free. Below him lay the world threaded with the bright tracks of a thousand possible journeys. The west wind came alongside him as he flew. A salt taste came into the air.

"You choose!" said the pet shop man. "It's your first journey. I'll come as far as the beach with you to see you on your way. You'll meet other travellers, of course, but even when you don't you'll never be lonely, for a journey is all the companion a true traveller needs."

So Sam flew off on the first of his great journeys. He was a boy with somewhere to go and able, at last, to go there, and as he flew the sun shone down on him and turned him from a boy in grey to a traveller of gold.

ABOUT THE AUTHOR

Margaret Mahy was born in Whakatane, New Zealand, the eldest of five children. She published her first story in a local newspaper at the age of seven.

She began work as a librarian whilst writing stories – but because she didn't write about New Zealand settings at the time, her work was rejected by New Zealand publishers. In 1968, an American editor discovered her work, asked to see all her stories and very soon after, published Margaret's first five picture books simultaneously.

In the 1970s, Margaret began writing junior novels and in the 1980s published older and then teenage fiction, including *The Haunting* and *The Changeover*, both of which won the Carnegie Medal.

Now Margaret writes for children of all ages, from her home in Governor's Bay.

Other White Wolves titles you might enjoy ...

Sky Ship and Other Stories
by Geraldine McCaughrean

Geraldine McCaughrean has won many awards for stories set in the past. Here are five brilliant tales that will transport you to times and places you will never forget.

Snow Horse and Other Stories
by Joan Aiken

Ghosts from the past inhabit the present in strange and frightening ways in these five memorable, spine-tingling stories from the classic writer of suspense fiction.

 # White Wolves